Alba
and the
OCEAN CLEANUP
LARA HAWTHORNE

**For family and friends on Claremont Road
and the Hamilton House Coexist community**

First U.S. edition 2020
First published in the U.K. in 2019 by Big Picture Press

Library of Congress Catalog Card Number pending
ISBN 978-1-5362-1044-6

19 20 21 22 23 24 TWP 10 9 8 7 6 5 4 3 2 1

Printed in Johor Bahru, Malaysia

This book was typeset in PiS Creatinin Pro.
The illustrations were done in watercolor and gouache and amended digitally.

BIG PICTURE PRESS
an imprint of
Candlewick Press
99 Dover Street
Somerville, Massachusetts 02144

www.candlewick.com

Alba
and the
OCEAN CLEANUP

LARA HAWTHORNE

BPP

There was once a small, quiet town
that overlooked a brilliant blue ocean.

And beneath the surface of
the warm, shallow water . . .

there was a beautiful reef.
Shimmering fish darted and dived, and strange
creatures scuttled into hidden places.

Amid the hubbub was a young
orange fish named Alba, who lived
next to an old spotted shell.

Every year on her birthday, Alba
found herself something special.

She loved things that were
spotted, striped, and round . . .

bumpy, spiky,
and bright . . .

or curvy, swirly,
and small.

Over the years she
grew and grew . . .

and so did her wonderful collection.

But as time went by, Alba found fewer beautiful objects . . .

and slowly, more trash started to appear.

Alba watched the reef change . . .

and every year more of her friends left.

One year on her birthday, Alba had no one to celebrate with. And though she searched and searched, she couldn't find a single beautiful thing for her collection. There was only garbage.

But Alba was determined. She kept looking until she was farther from home than she'd ever been.

Suddenly she noticed something glowing in the darkness. It was a pearl. "How wonderful!" Alba exclaimed.

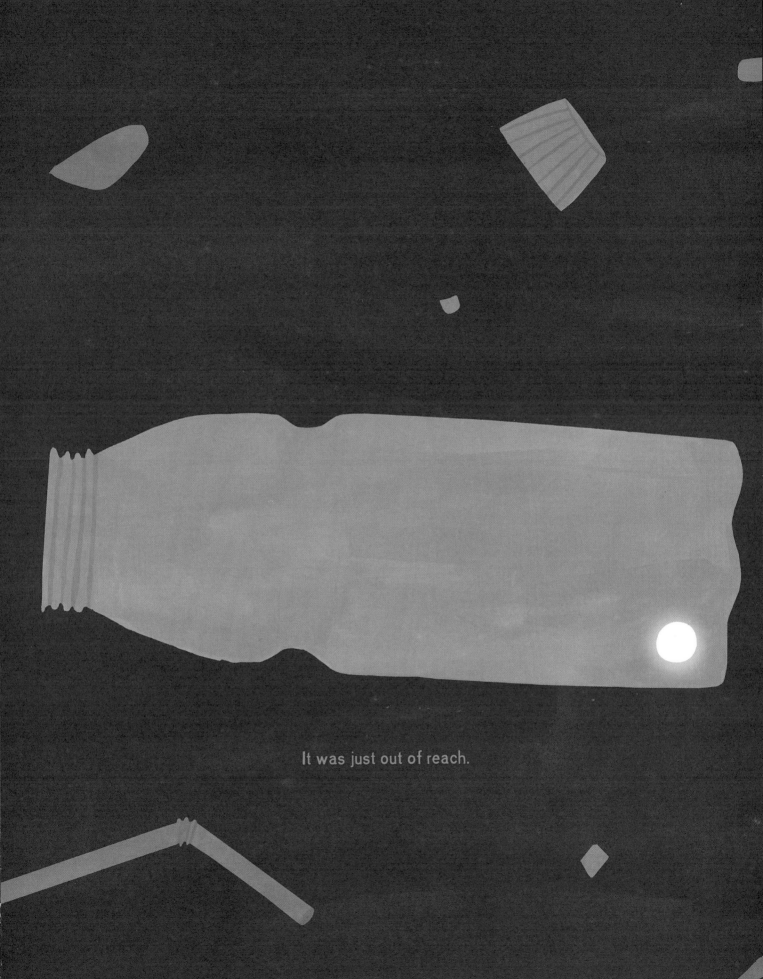

It was just out of reach.

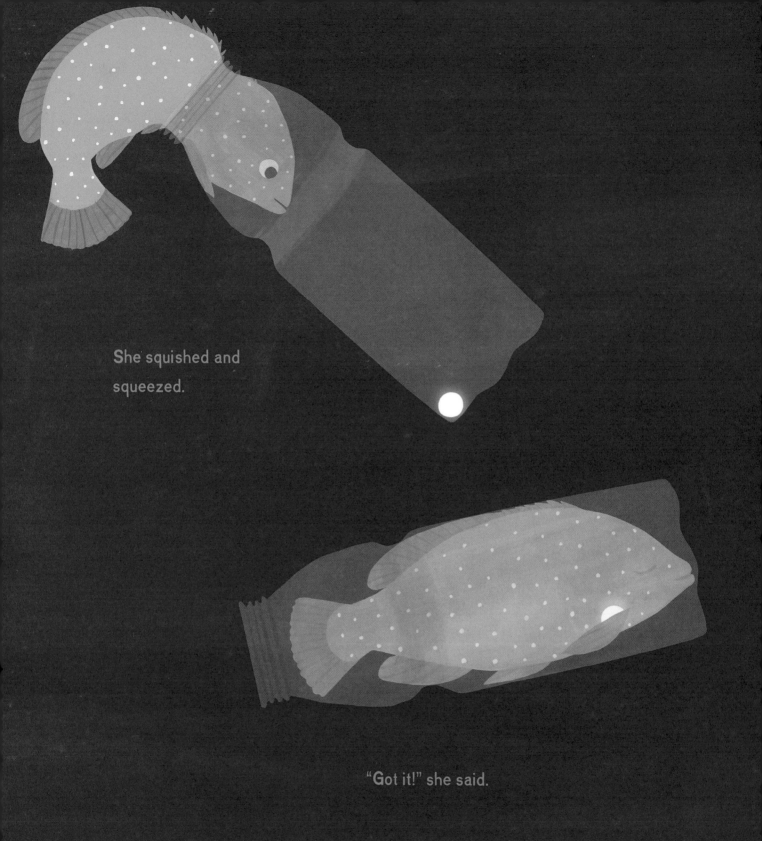

She squished and
squeezed.

"Got it!" she said.

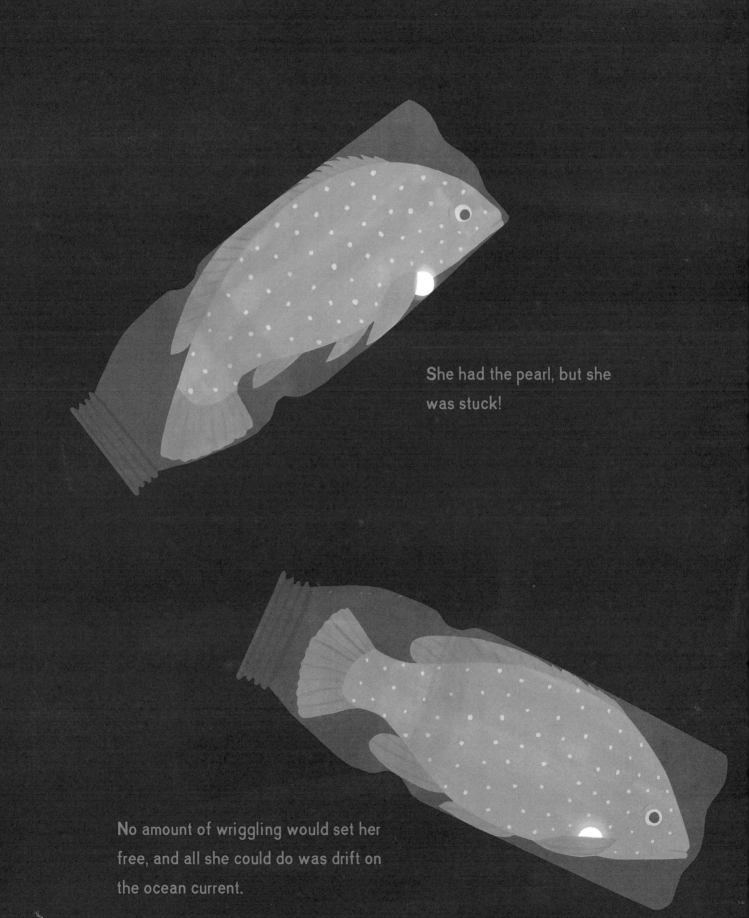

She had the pearl, but she was stuck!

No amount of wriggling would set her free, and all she could do was drift on the ocean current.

Eventually, Alba floated to the surface, where a peculiar
new world appeared. Giant boats moved on the surface
of the water, and white lights shone from the land through
the darkness.

Alba also saw a lot of trash.

She longed to go home. That night
she dreamed of her old spotted shell
nestled in the reef.

The next morning, a girl named **Kaia** was walking along the beach, looking for beautiful objects for her collection. She found Alba.

"Oh, no," Kaia said. "I'll get you out." And she did. Then she looked at all the plastic bottles and bags. "Our trash is everywhere," Kaia said.

"It's not safe for you," she said to Alba, and put her in a bucket of clean seawater.

"We've got to clean this up."

Kaia told everyone she met about Alba and about how dangerous their plastic and trash were making the oceans. They needed to make big changes.

The whole town worked together to clean up
the mess they had made. They cleaned and
cleaned and bit by bit, piece by piece, the
sea started to get a little safer again.

Soon the ocean was clean enough for **Alba** to return.
Kaia said goodbye and released her back into the water.

Still clutching her precious pearl, Alba went home to her spotted shell and her collection of treasures.

When she got there, she found that most of the trash was gone!

On Alba's birthday, she celebrated with her friends in the reef, which was becoming busy and bright again.

Alba's pearl dazzled her friends. As they gathered around, she told them the story of a brave girl named Kaia who had worked very hard to make their ocean clean again.

Did you spot . . . ?

Oceans are home to some of the most colorful and unique wildlife in the world. Go back through the book and see if you can spot some of Alba's ocean friends.

SPOTTED MORAY EEL
(Gymnothorax moringa)

Rocky surfaces with hidden crevices are the ideal locations for this snake-like creature to hide in. A solitary hunter, the spotted moray eel has poor eyesight but an excellent sense of smell and a painful bite.

BLUE-CHEEKED BUTTERFLYFISH
(Chaetodon semilarvatus)

A common sight on coral reefs, these striking fish mate with one partner for life, so they are often seen swimming in pairs. Their tiny snout helps them poke around for their food: coral polyps and small worms.

RED-SPOTTED CORAL CRAB
(Trapezia tigrina)

Don't be fooled by this crab's bright, beautiful polka dots. These feisty crustaceans fiercely guard their coral reef homes.

EMPEROR ANGELFISH
(Pomacanthus imperator)

This flat-bodied fish feeds on algae and sponges. As it grows into an adult, the patterns on its body become a light yellowish green, edged with vibrant electric blue.

GREATER BLUE-RINGED OCTOPUS
(Hapalochlaena lunulata)

The vibrant patterns on these tiny octopuses warn predators to stay away— they are highly venomous. They live in burrows on the ocean floor.

PINK DORID NUDIBRANCH

(Chromodoris bullocki)

Nudibranches are among the most stunning species of sea slugs in the world. Their vivid colors and textures enable them to blend in with their coral reef surroundings.

VIOLET-SPOTTED REEF LOBSTER

(Enoplometopus debelius)

This beautifully patterned reef lobster grows to be only about 15 centimeters/ 6 inches long. It lives in warm, tropical oceans near rocky surfaces and comes out to hunt at night.

LEAFY SEA DRAGON

(Phycodurus eques)

This seahorse cousin looks just like seaweed and is perfectly suited to the kelp forests in which it lives. The male leafy sea dragon looks after the babies, known as fry.

BLUE SEA STAR

(Linckia laevigata)

With arms covered in suckers, this sea star creeps along the ocean floor, attaching itself to rocks and coral.

OCELLARIS CLOWN FISH

(Amphiprion ocellaris)

These little fish can be found only on coral reefs. They live among the tentacles of sea anemones and have a mucus layer that protects them from the anemones' stings.

Taking Care of Our Oceans

Most people use plastic nearly every day, but it can be harmful to our environment. Plastic isn't biodegradable, which means it won't break down into smaller pieces, as some other materials do. It can stick around for hundreds of years.

When plastic ends up in the ocean, it can harm the animals that live there. Plastic bags can be mistaken for jellyfish and eaten by whales and turtles. Smaller creatures can choke on plastic straws, and small bits of plastic can be eaten by fish or seabirds. There are lots of ways we can look after our oceans. Here are a few things you can do to help:

1. Avoid using plastic products.

2. Always pick up any trash you see at the beach.

3. Never pour harmful chemicals down the drain.

4. Reduce, reuse, and recycle.

5. Encourage your community to do the same.

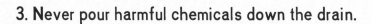

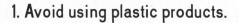